THE PARANORMAL

A True Story.

Copyright © 2020 Pavi Devaharan
All rights reserved.

CHAPTER ONE: WHERE IT ALL BEGAN.

1996, In a place deep down the mountains.

The story is set in a small village towards the outskirts of Germany. It was a town that had lots of natural and rare gemstone deposits. The gems were a primary source of the town's income as they were mined and sold to buyers around, it made us stand out and attract a lot of tourists. The village itself had an approximate population of about twenty-eight thousand people. As you can imagine, with a population size that small there wasn't much happening in our village.

We have the occasional carnival each year where we all line up in the middle of the main street and enjoyed the parade. It's probably the only time when our city looked busy and genuinely felt like there were other people around. Since I was still a kid at that point I'd be drooling away as the people from the parade throw packets of sugary goodness to us. It sometimes does turn into a challenge as we all fight for the chocolates and sweets shot across to us, luckily all the grownups around me helped out to fill my goody bag.

Another tradition that we had every year was "Laternelaufen", we usually celebrate this near St Martins Day. The city excitedly waits until 6pm as the blustering sun goes down, as soon as the day falls, we all gather together in the centre of our city. Like a stampede of fireflies, you'd see the whole town holding up a bright red lantern and letting them fly into the darkness of the night.

My family initially lived in a flat just above an Aldi store; when I was born, they decided to look for another house. It was crucial that wherever we moved, the place itself has to have a mansion feel to it, in fact it was my parents dream to; a dream that sadly came true. This is when they came across the house, The Burgasse House. After viewing several properties their eyes were fixed on one building and one building only, it was the building in the mountains. The property itself was strikingly huge and was split into 3 different compartments.

The house was a beige coloured building with cracked walls, blue coloured gates and a mysterious carving on a stone tablet that was hanging against on the wall. To this day it feels like an unsolved puzzle not knowing what was scripted on the ancient looking slate. Unlike most houses we had our stairs outside, the stairs led to each compartment. All 3 floors were used for different purposes however, we spent most of our time in the middle one. The staircases, themselves, were distinctly uneven. Majority of the stairs were just rubbles; the concrete was worn out which probably reflects the actual age of the house. Living on top of a mountain was no easy task, just to get up to the house you would have to climb approximately 100-200 stairs. In daylight you will have the most amazing view of the city however by night-time the whole atmosphere becomes sinister. The stairs become less visible, with only one dull lamppost illuminating the shadows of 200 stairs, accompanied with screeching insects that break the daunting silence on your journey up. The walls were infested with ivy plants that were growing out of control and knocking against the eroded concrete as the wind blows.

It wasn't a normal house, nothing was normal.

It was a gusty autumns day, and I had just finished school and my mum was ready to pick me up. As per any other day we walk up the stairs towards our house, but today was different. The crumbling stairs nearly made me slip as my mum tightly grips on to my hand to keep me on my feet. We now approached the gate, but again something wasn't right...

From a distance I seen my Dad, but he looked agitated and disturbed. He locked eyes with us and took a deep breath

"Don't come closer" he shouted.

We got startled, it was unusual to see my Dad shout. It took me a while, but I finally noticed a rough looking broom stick being swung against the floor. I took a couple more steps up the stairs as I curiously tried to look at why Dad told us to stop. I seen it...

It was only a glimpse but that's all it took for me to get shivers up my spine. It was at least 6ft long, and it was slithering across the ground whilst my Dad was trying to defend himself with nothing more than a broomstick. There was a trail of it's scaley skin whilst it was ping ponging across from left to right. I could only imagine that one wrong move will provoke it to leave an unforgettable bite, it would have been game over. Eventually, Dad managed to get the snake off our property, however, from the way it left it certainly felt like we haven't seen the last of that vicious floor dweller.

It didn't stop there, we always had slimy frogs, squatting in our front patio that gaze at you with undivided concentration when you take the stairs to go to the middle compartment. It was a unique experience to live there which is why it's so exciting to tell the story to people, the house was far from the ordinary. The wildlife was crazy, the building felt like it was falling apart and the night times felt like nightmares. During the course of this book, I'll unravel the true story of the house in the mountain, it's darkest secrets.

The house had some perks to it...

Despite stunning views and an aromatic atmosphere, we still regularly felt alienated in a way. Separated from the world. Not only from the world and community around us, but also from the larger world out there. Like we were in it, yet we were not. We had neighbours but we lived quite distantly from them as well. Not totally as per physical distance, but in matters of interaction. There was never a time we attempted to connect with them. We just knew they were there in the corner minding their own business. We get the occasional "Guten Morgen" but it was never really a proper conversation as such.

At this point of the story I was just an 8-year-old kid and as per most childhoods me and my friends played the usual: Pokémon, Yu-Gi-Oh and Beyblade. I went to a school which was a 40 minutes' walk from my house. The one place I felt a bit safer, I was constantly surrounded by my friends which pretty much distracted me from thinking about anything else. I always try my best to avoid looking at the time, it was my way to postpone the inevitable.

"Ding! Ding!" a spearing bell sound vibrates through my eardrums

"Dam !!"

I knew that only meant one thing…

It's 3 30, it all starts again. I get home and in desperation watch the big second hand chase the little minute hand. It felt like everything was going into slow motion as soon as I step into the house. Any opportunity not to be alone in a room, I'd take it without a second thought. I would constantly seek attention from my parents or my siblings, anything, anything at all just not to be alone.

The only question was, what terror awaits me?

What unease is "**it**" going to bring to my life?...

The age gap between me and my siblings was 5 to 6 years, my sister was the eldest followed by my brother who was one year younger than her. Due to the age gap we always had school at different times, by the time I joined primary school they were already in secondary. They wake up earlier then me and come back from school later then me. I wasn't the only one who felt this mischievous presence around me, my siblings felt the same, only problem was... we never talked about it. As I was the youngest, I wasn't left alone for too long, there was always someone around me even if it was just in another room.

The middle compartment was where we lived and spent most of our time in. The vintage looking kitchen was narrow, as disturbing as it sounds, we did have a few mice running around. The scattering of mouse traps is something I re-call very clearly. We either wake up to a dead mouse, or hear screaming on the occasional morning; since me and my siblings were still young, that's pretty much the best offensive strategy we could do when we have a showdown with a mouse. They did eventually go but it did take some time.

During this era we owned a navy-blue chunky TV which at that point was keeping current with technology. It made a high pitch frequency sound every time you turned it on, followed by the sound of discrepancy as it displays a black and white scramble before it tries to tune into a channel.

Creaky floorboards, light brown carpet, wooden walls...despite having its downsides the house was huge. Every hour we had the city clock clunking at us and since we lived so high up the breeze was amazing and calming, little did we know there was a massive storm ahead of us.

As soon as you enter the living room, you will see the kitchen on the left, walk 4 steps forward you will see my siblings' room and just with a couple more steps ahead you will see my parents room. The living room and my parents' room were separated by a massive wooden board nailed to the frame. We also had a small window, about the size of a 21" monitor in my parents' room that shoots beams of sunlight on the occasional good day; it had a net just to make sure no one carelessly attempts to jump out, we were kids after all.

Having blabbered on for a good two or three pages, you are probably wondering why I am writing this book. The answers to what was so unusual and paranormal about our large, tormented house in the mountains of a ghostly village.

What was I so afraid off??

I am going to share with you a series of events that have occurred in that house. Events that have proven to us that absolutely nothing short of the paranormal had existed there while we lived there.

Let the horror begin

CHAPTER TWO: THE FORBIDDEN FLOOR

The atmosphere around the house can sometimes disperse a vibe of pure monstrosity, wickedness... Frankly enough, I don't believe those words even begin to describe the extent of the pure evil aura that took hostage of that particular area of our town.

As the years progressed on, and as we got older, we slowly began to use all three floors for various reasons and purposes.

The top compartment was where we had the computer set up. One side of the room was filled with old toys, chairs and other rubbish, it just gathered dust. There was just enough room to fit in our computer with an obstacle free pathway to the front door. My brother and I were really into games, so we did hog that room more than others. If anyone remembers playing the game Rayman, consider me and my brother veterans. We literally played that game day and night.

I was 5 years younger than my brother, he used to think of any excuse possible to take my turn, the curious little me seen that as an opportunity. I made sure to fully make use of it and ask for things in return. By this point we can agree our house looked abnormal, but what if I told you there was more. The computer room had another level to it, the stairs were inside yet my dad had always said we were never allowed to go there. When you get told you can't do something it provokes you to want to do it more, that's what happened. The deal I made with my brother was, if he takes me upstairs and shows me what's up there, he can take my turn.

Another 10 minutes later my brother loses, it was showtime. The moment soon approached, before we took our first few steps towards the staircase, my brother suddenly stopped and made me promise this...

"Don't. Tell. Dad."

The excitement engulfed me, my legs started tingling and I couldn't stop smiling. I finally get to see what's on the other side of this mysterious staircase and what secrets lie upon us. We now meet head to head with the first step, just before making that first move me and my brother look at each other one last time with hesitation. We didn't know whether it was the right thing to do, maybe Dad didn't let us go there for a reason. We came this far; it was too late to turn back. With caution we make our way to the top floor, taking each step carefully to avoid making the slightest sound.

(deep panting)

I was finally here, I made it. Slowly my inner voice whispered to me, making me re-think everything. I should not be here!! The first door was shut and locked with a rusty padlock covered in dirt. Straight away a million questions started striking into my thoughts.

The door felt like it was getting larger and larger as I was staring at it. I gently knock against the beat-up brown door. Between each knock the only response I got was the gathered dust spreading into the air like a lump of smoke. But all of a sudden, within that 10 second timeframe of total silence I heard something, soon later I knew it was "it" that I heard.

"PAVI!!!" my brother exclaimed

"What on earth are you doing, DO NOT TOUCH ANYTHING"

At this point all my brother was stressing about was not getting caught by Dad, if we did, it would have been all on his head because he was the older one.

After my brother's outburst I resisted my temptation to knock again and slowly started moving forward. Surprisingly, the second room was wide open, it was infested with spider webs and had a stained old micky mouse ball and an unsteady rocky chair laying on broken floorboards. We felt like even taking one step into that room might make us fall right through to the computer room so we didn't risk it.

We soon approached the last door which was already a third open.

Just as me and my brother try to fully open it, we hear noticeable footsteps.

"***Clomp... Clomp***"

My heart starts raising, sweat starts dripping from my nose... we needed to get out of here. Now!

My dad was on his way to the top floor, me and my brother scurried down trying not to leave any evidence behind of us ever being there.

We failed...

With all the rush I accidentally stumbled upon the toolbox on the staircase, a clear sign that my dad immediately picked up on. With steams coming out of his head, he got both of us and told us off for going up there.

"You are NOT allowed to go upstairs; do I make myself clear?" my dad yelled

With guilt, me and my brother had nothing to say back, we simultaneously nodded yes and hoped that's the only telling off we were going to get that day. However, it did bug me for the remainder of the day, what was behind that locked door, I feel like the answer to that question cleared up as we lived longer in that house.

CHAPTER THREE: THE EYES FROM THE ABOVE

After living at the house for a few years my dad decided to renovate the bottom floor, giving it a facelift and made it to look really good. We added various homey and cosy essentials every family needed. After the renovations, the entire floor looked modernized and classy.

Eventually we started using the bottom floor more and soon became everyone's favourite compartment and everyone spent most of their time there. The main luxury of being downstairs was both the enormous kitchen and the bathroom. The bathroom was humongous, it was double the size of our living hall. As you carry on walking, there was one more room as you pass the living hall which had a lot of space, probably the best room to get a breath-taking view of our city. The top floor had its own front garden where my mum grew a lot of vegetation and luscious flowers, mainly roses. To prevent anyone from accidently falling off, we had a rusty barrier gate. You now have decent understanding on the layout and hopefully a good image on how our house looked like. Now for the events

The house had problems... many problems...

One was The Eyes. What were these eyes? I don't know. It's been years but up to this day, I can't answer that question. It was a cold winters day, frost was building up in layers above our crumbled staircase. I was heading down to join my family downstairs, however out of all days I wished I didn't wake up late on this one. As I transition from my room towards the entrance door, I immediately seen the lights flickering. At this point I made myself believe the lights always flickered like this so I didn't think much and carried on.

"Slam"

I shut the door, and without sparing a second the creeping

coldness starts drying my skin out. I turn and look down the stairs.

"Dam"

It felt like déjà vu, in my head I started having dark violins play a slow horror melody as I gaze down the stairs fully knowing what is going to happen. All I know is that every time I took the stairs from the middle floor heading to the bottom, I had and felt an ominous sensation, a presence of something other than me.

It was like something inside was nudging me, telling me that I was being followed and that this something was right behind me. I would turn back really quickly, and there would be nothing. Every time. Several times I had that feeling and always, I turned back to nothing, to an empty normal space behind me. But then I would move forward and the feeling would return. The sensation refused to go away. It was like warning bells were ringing loudly in my body, like every single hair on my body was standing on end.

With hesitations I walk down the first 4 steps trying to hold my balance on the icy surface. I made it one third of the way down when this happened.

I saw something, something in the corner of my eye. The dark violin noises gradually got louder in my head; I tried to tilt my neck to see what it was but my body refused to listen to me. It wasn't the first time this happened..

Every time I took those stairs, I would see something pillared right in middle of our top garden. These things were never up-front and confrontational. I would simply notice them from the sides of my eyes. It was hard to tell what it really was, the only way I could describe it is a shadow standing smack in the middle of the garden, just there. My skin would crawl and goose bumps would break out each time. It was sheer terrifying. I never would see a thing when I turned around to face it squarely only when I looked away partially. No matter how fast I try to go down the stairs it feels like for a brief moment I enter a whole new realm where time decides to freeze, and right then, is when the demonic presence tries to take me hostage. The air around, always had a kind of weird sense to it. And it only, only happened when I was going down the stairs.

It was hard to tell if there was actually someone or something crawling up behind me or if I was simply imagining things. But still the sensation stayed, and it felt totally real. Knowing it wasn't only when it was night, but also in broad daylight just makes the whole situation so much more unescapable.

These recurring events never seemed to stop; it was a never-ending cycle. The fear in me grew and grew and eventually it got to a point where I'd jump the last 5 stairs, and soon it became a new normal. I always jumped.

Every time.

I didn't want whatever was chasing me to reach me, the utter thought of this devilish presence touching me made my stomach turn. I always thought, I'd either get pushed down the stairs or get caught and be detained some place where no one can find me.

It was a very scary experience to have as a child. It's human nature to feel nervous and cautious when you encounter something you can't explain in words, the fear in the sensation, the fear of the unknown - whatever it was that lurked in the shadows of our house, made me dread the staircase.

And it did repeat itself. The shadow was always there.

Years later, after my siblings and I had moved to the U.K., I brought up the conversation and finally opened up about those strange encounters and they, my siblings, were startled. This was the moment I found out I was not going through this on my own. They both started telling me about their own stories and the experiences they had while we had lived in the house. It just made me think, if only I spoke to them sooner I wouldn't have been as scared as I was when I was younger, maybe I would have had the courage to genuinely find out what it was rather then running away from it.

We talked about it and thoroughly broke down what we had individually seen and felt. I understood that they might have thought they were imagining things and that if they came forward with those stories and spoke up about them, nobody would believe them and they would, instead, get taunted endlessly because of it. That was my fear too. It was why we never talked about it until we had relocated to the U.K.

It had been relieving, a bit, to know that I had not been alone in my struggles with the creepiness at that house.

Nowhere else did these strange and discomfiting occurrences occur. It also does not explain in any way the fact that my siblings had similar experiences too.

CHAPTER FOUR: THE BATTLE OF BANGS

The upcoming event happened a couple of years later. This event was paranormal and skin crawling in its every right. This one proved to be much different from all other events, in every story so far there might have been realistic explanations but for this it was indescribable. The nervousness this memory constantly haunts out of me is the main reason I'm choosing to talk about this now.

From my previous stories, you can tell that I usually experienced the creepy happenings and encounters only when I was alone. In this incident, however, I was with my brother. This was also the event that made me a bit more comfortable telling people my story, if there is only one person anything can be said but if two people experienced the same thing it's a whole different scenario.

One thing both me and my brother had in common is the love for playing games. During this time, the PlayStation 2 was trending and as per any kid we wanted it. My dad eventually managed to buy it for us and from that day onwards we were glued to our chairs.

It was a relaxing Sunday afternoon; the birds were chirping the surrounding buildings were glistening as the sun was illuminating the city with its positive rays of sunshine's. It was the perfect day to kickstart our journey on this new console exploring the endless fun and joy the gaming world had to offer. Well that's what we thought at least.

My parents had headed out with my sister. It was grocery shopping day, so they left around mid-day to make sure the food wasn't wiped out from the shelves. It was typical for me and my brother to stay behind because both of us can't stand it to be in a shop for more than 5 minutes, in fact, our priority was to make sure we complete the new games as fast as possible so we can move on to the next one.

Both of us had sat transfixed to the chunky screen and to our consoles playing our lives away, totally oblivious of the passing of time. We were so absorbed into the game, it felt like we were held captive by this amazing masterpiece. The room had been still and quiet besides the noise from our keys and our breathing, and occasional yells of surprise, taunt or victory.

I was being crushed by my brother on the 1 vs 1 battles, but I managed to turn the table around after a good 20minutes of gameplay. It felt like the student has finally become the master as I was beating my brother in each battle then onwards.

A few long minutes into serious gaming, everything started going south. The distinct noises of two people suddenly became 3. It was faint at first but then it became more and more noticeable. We started hearing subtle noises coming from the direction of the rigid board. The noises were persistent, it felt like someone was gradually getting angrier and angrier, the tone of the bangs slowly started scaling up. My brother and I noticed it but did not attribute it to anything sinister. We assumed it was a draft of wind that might have gotten in through open windows or any other trivial and unimportant reason.

Time went on and the banging got more aggressive. Suddenly, it began to sound more human-like. Like a person was pounding or hitting the board with all their fury and anger. At this point, we could not excuse away the banging or chalk it up as something else. With fear, my sweaty fingertips slowly edged towards the pause button on the controller. We tried to look brave, but the sound was totally rattling us to our cores. I knew how I was feeling, and I knew my brother was not feeling any better. We were terrified. Sweat had poked out of me and they had trickled down in their numbers. The tenseness made my temperature rise rapidly even though the room itself was airy. My heart was thumping, in the small intervals of the banging where it was dead quiet, I could hear my brothers was too.

Since my brother was the eldest person present, he automatically felt it was his duty to protect me and keep me safe from whatever was behind that board causing all the commotion. It didn't even occur to me to argue it out with him. At that point, I felt I needed all the help and protection I could get.

My brother had searched around and picked up a power twister. This power twister was essentially a metal spring bar. He was nervous. He was scared. He knew he was approaching uncertainty.

He slowly crept his way up to the side of the board with it. I knew my brother was going through the same hurricane of emotions, and so I really admired the high level of courage and tenacity he showed. Step by step he steadily walked down to our side of the board and banged back with brute force.

"..."

Silence.

The banging on the other side had suddenly stopped. Just like that. It was almost like a tap had been turned off. The battle had been won the second it had begun.

My brother had turned to look at me. It was very weird, but we had relaxed a bit even though our nerves were still taut. The fact that the banging had stopped must have boosted us a bit psychologically, made us feel like we could control the situation no matter what the circumstance actually was. We had stood stonily, without making a sound or saying a word, to listen for anything, even a flutter from the other side of the board.

A few minutes after my brother's stirring display of courage, there was a loud sound.

'Smack!'

It sounded like the board itself nearly cracked with the cheer force of the beast that we provoked, both of us were startled and stopped breathing. The banging started up again just as it had before my brother's disturbance. The fear that had dissipated out of our spirits had come crashing like the waves. Our hearts had pummelled with each bang. We were completely at our wits end; we were so riled up with fear that we scrambled down to the phone to call our parents. We knew this situation was something bigger than both of us and we couldn't handle it on our own. My brother rang my parents and spoke to them, stuttering to even get a full clear word out; fear written all over his face and voice. We patiently sat on the chair, starstruck, defenceless, praying they come home quickly. It's as if we were a small vulnerable insect stuck in a web, unable to move due to fright, being hunted by this invisible enemy that we claimed to be "the paranormal".

Within minutes my dad arrived with my mum and sister, anxiously running towards us making sure we were okay. My dad definitely assumed the worst, there is no way he would have arrived this quickly without stepping on the pedal, considering the distance he had to cover from our house to the shop. The noises ceased immediately, with their arrival. Both my parents were relieved to see us still in one piece, they assumed there was a robber who broke into the house. My dad was so agitated he searched through all the rooms looking for the villain behind the ruckus and disturbance, he clenched his fist just to be ready for anything that springs from the shadow. In the meantime, my mum and sister stayed by us and interrogated us with persistent questions.

My father looked around the whole middle floor, there was nothing, everything had seemed normal. There was no trace of anything being there, nothing at all. He checked the windows thoroughly and said it had been shut and there was nothing around on the other side of the board that could have possibly made all those repeated noises. And there was nothing in the whole house that would have had the initiative to stop when my brother banged the board.

That was a very terrifying incident that I still think about. No one can explain what had occurred to this day.

Still you could be asking in your mind: "Are you really, really sure it had not been the wind slamming against that board or that a burglar had not been trying to break in?"

No chance. The window was too small, and it was fully netted, more importantly it was closed. There was a good 5 meters distance between the actual window and the board itself. No draft would be powerful enough to blow through and gather enough strength to pound on the board the way it had been pounded that day. The worst thing is, it wasn't even windy that day yet alone assuming the source of the slamming sound was caused by the window.

It also was definitely not a burglar. There was no way such an intruder would have come in except through the door. We live in the mountains, and for someone to be able to get into the top compartment and the middle one without using the stairs and the door, they would have had to have flown in. If you look down the window, from that particular room there is a 20-meter drop, essentially there is no human who could have come in through that way, it was unrealistic and impossible.

Furthermore, there was no single rip on the window net, no avenue or opening for a rush of air to push in and make the sounds that had been made.

Up until this day, this is probably the only story that stuck by me. It was the main one which genuinely made me think it wasn't me imagining anything, and that there really was something creepy floating around our house because both me and my brother experienced it.

CHAPTER THREE: THE UNINVITED GUEST

The calendar had moved and crept slowly to my brother's birthday. Even though we lived in a small harmonious town we had a lot of friends and family living nearby. As per all parties the countdown for prepping started as soon as we woke up. Like a flock of busy bees everyone was buzzing around the house to get everything ready, and the mayhem began. We usually host the parties downstairs because we were able to fit more guests in. As the mouth-watering scent of my mum's cooking overwhelmed the house, we started getting guests come through and everyone was getting into the party mode. Our birthday parties followed a simple schedule, we wait for all the guests to arrive, cut the cake, play some games and start serving food to everyone. We usually play hide and seek which was fun but playing it in our house was a whole new story. I'd hide but wished someone found me first just to avoid being on my own.

We cut the cake and played a few games, and now for the main part people were waiting for, it's munch time. We had a lot of guests over, so we usually get recyclable cutlery on occasions like this, and this is where everything went sideways. My mum approached me and asked me to go to the middle floor to grab some spoons and plates.

I briefly look out the window and it felt like the whole world changed...

Heavy dark grey clouds gathered together covering every inch of the sky, followed by short bursts of lightening that shacked the whole atmosphere. Birds that were sitting on our roof top flew out as if they were running away from something. The odd slimy frog that visits us daily was laying on our front patio, however strangely it wasn't looking at us for a change, it's googly stare was reverted to our middle floor.

"It" was here.

The visitor no one had invited, and I had not anticipated. With hesitation I slowly made my way towards the rusty door to go outside. Never has the door seemed further away, maybe the doubtfulness got the better of me and made the walk to the door an endless blackhole. A few minutes which felt like an eternity later, I finally got to the door. I told myself…

"Come on, just get it over and done with."

I had opened the door and stepped out with some trepidation. With distress I walked slowly up the stairs.

Clunk! Clunk!

Our city clock clank through the tensed air marking the time of 8'o clock, the beginning of nightfall. Each step I took then onwards felt like I was walking on quicksand, even though my brain wanted to move my legs had its mind of its own resisting each step I wanted to take. I had tried my best to be brave, look straight ahead and march up the stairs with determination. When I got to the middle floor of our building without any strange encounter or incidence, I had been so relieved, yet surprised at the same time. That feel, in itself, had not been expected.

After gathering all my courage, I stretched my hands out to turn the decayed knob on the door when I noticed something strange that immediately made me freeze up. A direful feeling just slithered into my body, the air got eerie and thick and made it feel like someone was strangling me as I struggle to get a gasp of air. I was in shock.

A portent smell started making its way up my runny nose, it was alerting every neuro nerve in my brain that something bad was going to happen. This wasn't normal, the smell was getting worse by the second. It was like a pile of dead bodies that were left to rot for a couple of years. With all that frightfulness I finally realized why my body was trembling on its feet.

"It" was there…

The door to the middle floor was opaque, you could see what's happening inside however it was blurry. I felt like all my senses were heightened, I could hear the smallest creak of the floorboards and see everything with brightened colours. My body set off my survival instinct as I gazed through the door when I saw "it", the uninvited guest.

As I stared through the door, I couldn't believe my eyes…

A snow-white figure was gliding towards the window, trailing with it a long thick shadow which I could only assume was its hair. It was around 5 foot 11 or 6 foot; all I knew at that instance was that it was double the size of me and it was after something. Its movements were distinctively gentle and slow, almost like it was trying to be subtle on purpose to look for something, or someone. As it edged towards the window its movement stopped. It's head slowly, slowly…slowly started rotating towards my direction as its hair was dragged along the floor.

I couldn't believe my eyes – is this real? I took a moment to pinch myself just to make sure I wasn't imagining it and truly hoped this was just a really bad nightmare. A pinch later nothing changed…it was still there staring out our window. I could see the curtains dancing away as the wind is gushing in from the outside. It did occur to me that it might have been a family member who for somewhat reason went upstairs. But it couldn't be it, this wickedness figure couldn't be human. It didn't resemble anyone I knew, nor did it's movements – it was like it was skating elegantly in a ring of ice in slow motion. The tension got the better of me, I had to see this through, I can't go back empty handed. I twist the door handle ever so carefully trying to avoid the slightest sound, inevitably the old handle produced a mouse like squeak. My eyes were fixed on the figure, they were so dry that I could feel little cracks emerging from my pupils. I didn't want to lose sight of it. I open the door, ready to face whatever it was sheltering itself behind the doors.

When I peeped in, there was absolutely nothing and no one by the window – as always. Always nothing. This time, all I saw was the curtain billowing in the breeze.

At first, I had wanted to believe and put it down as a mere illusion or a trick played by the curtains and the light, but my logical mind denied me even that. I had seen a human like figure, and I know what I saw. The human figure had maintained shape and consistency till it got to the window. Hardly possible by a curtain being blown by the wind.

With caution I scout the whole room to make sure nothing is lurking that could do a surprise ambush. I rushed into the kitchen and pulled the draw handle. I took the cutlery and without a second thought I ran back downstairs.

At this point I wasn't sure it was a good idea to share this incident with my family… as always, I kept this to myself

CHAPTER FIVE: THE ONE WE LEFT BEHIND

After about nine to ten years of living in the mountains and with nature and wildlife, my parents decided to move to the U.K. It raised mixed feelings for me.

One part of me couldn't wait to leave this haunted house, on the hand, there is always going to be a sentimental bond for the city you were born in and all the friends you make. The pro's outweighed the con's by miles so I was genuinely excited and ready to embark on new adventures. It was an exciting move because we had a lot of our relatives that lived there already and the prospect of seeing them on a more regular basis, was thrilling. Living on a mountain to living in a normal house with neighbours around was definitely a big change for me.

From living a life with barely anyone around us to suddenly being around busy streets, family and friends visiting every day, it was good. I for one had been really nervous. I was the youngest, so most of my life, most of what I knew was built around our little village in the mountains. But even then, me along with everyone else in the family had been aching for a change of some sorts. The idea of moving to the UK had merely been a decision, a decision we spoke and hushed about, until we actually got to move. With a mind full of ambition, and a body full of excitement, we all had packed our things together and moved out of the little town in Germany that had given memories of all sorts of to us.

Not all of us moved on that first day though. My dad had stayed behind to try to sell the house and make arrangements that would help our stay in the UK. It turned out that those details were not a walk in the park. It took a while for my dad to handle and sort them out, and so my dad had to stay for some time in Germany.

We left our dad behind with no one to accompany him, well,

that's what we thought. When you live in that house it never feels like you're alone, because no matter what…"it" will always be with you. My father was the one we had left behind, left at the mercy of who or whatever actually owned our home. All the stories so far, in some sense the whole family was still together, but the stuff my dad witnessed was on a different level.

Due to our move to the U.K. and to the fact that it was just him in the building, my dad had moved down to the bottom floor. As I mentioned, the bottom floor was newly renovated so compared to the middle floor this was like living in luxury. It was huge but in some ways I don't think that was a good thing, especially when you live on your own.

From all the stories I've been told by my dad, I could only gather the fact that he had too many sleepless nights. Every night he spent on the bottom floor had been a nuisance, even though it's the most comfortable place, it had its downfalls.

My dad as per any other day came back home after a hefty day at work; he was alone, so he usually takes food home from his workplace. As soon as he got to the bottom floor, he indulged himself with an Italian Mozzarella Pizza and was eating it on our glossy dining table in the kitchen. As he was finishing his last bite of the pizza he heard something.

"high pitch static noise"

It was the sound of our TV being switched on. Immediately my Dad got into offensive mode and started scouting around the house to see if anyone was there. There was no one.

He knew for a fact the TV was off when he walked in and sensed something wasn't right. At this point my Dad was already aware that we didn't live in a normal house, in some way he wasn't stunned to see what just had happened. He turned the TV off, turned the lights of and tried to get some sleep.

"KNOCK… KNOCK…KNOCK"

10 minutes into his sleep he heard a knocking noise. He was confused, no one would be visiting him at this time in the night, he woke up baffled and made his way to the door. Once again, he knew something wasn't right. Usually the front light shines if someone's at the door, this time it was pitch black. Being as careful as possible he slowly turns the door handle to see who it was.

Once again, nothing.

He put his shoes on to see if there was anyone nearby but no-one was around, it was just dead silence. He went back inside and attempts to sleep again. This time he heard sounds from the middle floor, as if someone is walking around.

"creak... creak"

It didn't stop, it felt like whatever it was made itself feel at home and kept walking up and down. This then started being a daily routine. Everyday he would hear noises on repeat. When I had seen my dad come to visit us in the UK I could barely recognize him, his eyes were just blacked out. He just looked hollow and his eyes were just covered in bags, the tiredness was just so visible. He could barely get any sleep or rest. Each time his eyes closed, they would spring open at a clatter or persistent scratch.

My dad, had enough, he took action. Another cold evening, it all started happening again. My dad comes back from work and watched a bit of TV. He hoped that he could finally get a break from all this and eventually get some peaceful sleep.

"**Gush**..."

Just as his eyes were shutting he hears the kitchen tap go off. He flinched in his seat and tried to snap out from his broken sleep. He rushes into the kitchen and see's the kitchen tap on full blast, this time he had enough.

Angrily, he walks back to the living hall and grabs a metal bar just ready for the next move. He didn't have to wait long...

The footsteps started all over again. Dad started banging back with the metal bar vigorously and tried to get whatever it was making the noise to disappear. He was furious and lost his temper… it got to a point where he was shouting, to some extent all he wanted to do is knockout this thing. My Dad always had been fearless in general. Surprisingly, whatever he did that day worked. From that point onwards he didn't hear any sounds or any paranormal stuff happening.

There was one other event which left a memorable mark with my dad. On this particular evening, he decided to go down to the cellar to take out the bins that were spilling over. It was almost dark, but he forgot to take them out earlier and it didn't cross his mind till late.

When he got into the cellar, he noticed there was a shadow-like figure there with him. It sort of loomed within a few meters of his sight. He could barely see it, being a shadow, but it appeared to be facing him. My dad did not pay it much attention at this point because it could've been anything or any random person. He ignored it and tried to focus on what had brought him down there. He turned around to the bins and tried to grab the handle of one. He looked back again out of sheer curiosity, only to find that the figure or shadow was no longer there or anywhere in the vicinity for that matter. He had not heard any sounds that suggested that someone had been leaving or exiting the cellar.

All these happenings and more, and we cannot still come up with a rational or scientific explanation for why they had occurred. Nothing realistic to explain away the eerie feeling the encounters gave us during and after the experience. The silent fear we lived in, feeling that anything could happen to us at any time, that dark forces could and may do me harm, was sheer terrifying.

CHAPTER 6 – OUR FINAL GOODBYE

All the stories which I have shared up until this point were based on my childhood, events which happened when I was fairly young. This one however happened at the beginning of 2018.

It was early January, usually a time where people start their years with hope and joy. Unfortunately, this wasn't the case for us. During this period both my uncle and aunty were admitted to the hospital, it was devastating. I always seen my uncle as a superhero, no matter what he did he gives us the warmth and confidence that anything can be accomplished. The stories he used tell us about his life in Sri Lanka really made me think of him as a role model, he was the definition of fearless. Seeing such a strong, bold man lying on a hospital bed really got me speechless

My aunty was admitted at the same hospital, but her ward was on the other side. She was definitely one of the kindest people I knew. She always said my name in a unique way which is something I'll never forget about her. It was her caring nature which made her so special to me and all of our other family members, and those memories of her will forever stay with us.

That week was a whole new experience, I've never really lost anyone who was dear to me and in one week I managed to lose two people. It got to a point where I've cried so much that I physically had no more tears to spare, I was in utter shock and disbelief.

How did all this happen so quickly and in such a short amount of time. My uncle passed away and a couple of days later my aunty passed. All of us were crushed to the core, and with a heartful of grief we eventually started organizing the funeral arrangements.

This was when it started getting a bit strange.

All our family members were making their way down to our city, people from all over the world gathered that day to show their condolence, it made me realize how many people's life's they have touched. The hardest part was telling my grandma that her son passed away, the worst thing was she had dementia… she found it really difficult to remember who even I was. Because no one knew how she was going to react; my other uncles and my dad didn't tell her all this happened because she is really fragile. The last thing they want is something happening to her as a result of passing on the news.

It was the day before the funeral and my uncle and his wife were bringing along my grandma to stay at a hotel before the funeral. Bear in mind my grandma is still oblivious to what actually happened. The journey to the hotel took approximately 2 hours, but a lot happened within that time.

This is how my uncle described the story to us…

It was a quiet drive on a winters evening, there was the occasional chitter chatter, but majority of the journey was complete silence. Everyone was too upset to really sustain a full conversation, partly because everyone was still grieving, and on the other hand, everyone was so worried how my grandma will take it once she finds out her eldest son passed away. It was a whirlpool of emotions and thoughts, but that's when this happened …

"araaro aryraaro, araaro aryraaroh"

My grandma scouts around the car to see where the noise is coming from, but she looked confused.

"araaro aryraaro, araaro aryraaroh".

This time she taps my uncle and asked whether he can hear someone singing a lullaby. At this point my uncle was lost for words and freaked out. He was so confused, to him all there was is complete silence, to reassure himself he asked his wife and she agreed. My uncle was so curious at this point. He asked her one question, this startled them all and kept them on the edge of their seat for the rest of the journey.

He asked,

"Amma, who does it sound like?".

She calmly replied, "it sounds like my oldest son".

With a stunt look my uncle tried to reel more information out of her but that's all she had. The thing which bugged everyone the most is that she had no idea that my uncle passed away and little did she know where she is even going in the car. For her to say what she said made everyone question everything, in a way we hoped it was true because we weren't ready to say our farewells to our uncle just yet.

A few days before; me, my sister and sister-in-law were downstairs reminiscing about both my uncle and aunty who passed away. We realized they both had their own motivational stories and thinking back they did go through a lot growing up. Slowly, we moved on to talking about spirits because a lot of other events happened by this point which raised this topic.

My sister in law is very sceptical when it comes to the paranormal, however after that day she did slowly believe in it. It was a tense topic and we started telling each other all these creepy stories, one of them being my aunty having a moment during my uncle's funeral where she genuinely acted possessed.

It was such a shock to see because never have I seen something like this, no one at all expected it. My uncles tried to calm her down, but she was someone else at this point. She literally had some superhuman strengths and managed to move free from both my uncles. Eventually, they managed to take her out of the room and she went unconscious for a while. As we were discussing that story we hear a loud noise from upstairs.

We thought it was the neighbours and we didn't think much of it. Slowly, the whole room started to get a bit colder. There was no draft, it just suddenly became really cold. My sister in law addressed this whilst we were in the middle of the conversation, both my sister and me agreed but again chose to ignore it. What happened next was hard to ignore…

As we carry on, the TV flashed, a bright beaming light projected out from the TV for literally a second. All 3 of us broke into silence and looked at each other to take into grasps what just happened. More than me and my sister, my sister in law was in complete and utter shock. She never really had anything happen in her life and even if something did happen, she usually would have a logical explanation to it. This time, like us, she was lost for words. I broke the ice by asking both of them…

"Did you see that, or did I just imagine this".

I was hoping they would say no but they both agreed they seen it, we were creeped out. It didn't feel comfortable anymore talking about spirits, we tried to change the topic to something else and tried to normalize what just happened.

The last story I would like to share with you is probably the one which genuinely gave me goosebumps as it happened. For this we will have to rewind back just one day before the funeral. After hearing my grandma, uncle and aunty arriving at the hotel me and my brother thought to go down to visit them. At this point me and my brother were genuinely worried about my grandma because no one has broken the news to her yet. We had to watch out what we say and make sure nothing slipped out. We give my uncle a ring who came down to guide us to their room. They were all there, my grandma 2 of my aunties and 2 of my uncles. Even though everyone was grieving we all came to an acceptance of what happened and eventually started talking as we would normally do.

My uncle was cracking jokes and soon everyone else was jumping in with the reminiscing and stories; everyone but my grandma. When I looked at her, she just looked confused and baffled and kept turning as if she was looking for something. At this point I didn't think anything of it. Eventually it was around 9pm and we thought to make moves to head home. As we were saying our bye's my grandma still looked puzzled and didn't respond to any of us, at this point everyone in the room knew something was up. My uncle asked her what was wrong.

She hesitantly raised her arm and pointed to the corner of the hotel room, she said she keeps hearing someone say "amma" from the corner of the room. Literally every hair on my body was standing upright, at a slow pace I rotate my head towards my brother and he looked equally as stunt. Everyone in the room couldn't believe what just happened. No one was anywhere near that corner the whole time we were in the room. It was just an open space. Even though everyone had a sense of fear as anyone would, we all wanted to know who's voice she heard. Again, my uncle tried to reel more information from her, but she just remained quiet.

This book entailed some of the most abnormal events which happened in my life. To be honest there might be logical explanations for each of the events however when you are faced with adversity it's hard to know what to think. A lot of people out there are very skeptical about the whole ideology of there being anything other than humans, to be honest I would have been the same. It takes personal experience to even open-up your mindset to consider there is something much bigger out there.

THE END.

Printed in Great Britain
by Amazon